ALIENS OUTFOXED

Vimaladhithan Balasubramanian

Art by Kanaga Priya S

In debt to God forever.

This book is dedicated to all kids who love to read and to all parents and grandparents who put their kids to sleep with a nice bedtime story.

This book belongs to

_____

Far away, on an alien planet called 'Planet Qurious', a teacher was talking to his students. There was an upcoming science exhibition in the school, and the teacher had selected 2 students, a boy alien named 'B' and a girl alien named 'G' to travel to a new planet (one that you may be well familiar with) – 'Planet Earth'.

Aliens B and G were instructed to capture, cage, and bring three unique pairs of adult and baby animals. The teacher alien told them that the baby animal would resemble the parent, but only be smaller. During the discussion with the teacher, Alien G had entered the below notes on her laptop as a pre-travel checklist,

1. Big spaceship with GPS (borrow from school)
2. Fill up the spaceship's fuel tank
3. Three cages for 3 pairs of animals (borrow from school)
4. Food and snacks for the journey
5. Take this laptop

B and G were excited to fly to Planet Earth and made the necessary arrangements.

B and G set the navigation on auto-pilot mode and enjoyed their space travel. They crossed the icy-cold Neptune (brrrr...), even colder Uranus (brrrrrrrrrrrr...), ringed Saturn, gigantic Jupiter, reddish Mars, and finally reached their destination – the blue planet, **Earth**.

The aliens set the engine to silent mode so that they could sneak up on the animals. They found a dog walking in a garden and pressed the ZAP button on the console to abduct it. The next moment, there was a dazzling ray of light from the spaceship and the poor unsuspecting dog was pulled upwards and into the spaceship.

The aliens were very happy with their first catch and B started talking to the dog and G brought her laptop to take notes.

"Good day, strange animal. I'm B and this is G, may I know who you are?", asked B. "I'm Mrs. Dog", replied the dog. "Pleased to meet you, Mrs. Dog! We are from planet Qurious and there's a science exhibition on our planet, for which we'll need to bring you and a baby dog for display. You'll be a star attraction there!", beamed B.

The aliens immediately locked her in a cage and Mrs. Dog became sad. G looked at the dog from top to bottom and jotted down the following notes on her laptop,

Baby dog checklist:
1. Bark with a 'woof woof' sound
2. Wag its small tail often
3. White-colored with brown patches

B and G started searching the neighborhood for a baby dog based on the checklist. It was a bright sunny day, and a baby dog was having fun playing with a ball in the park. The alien spaceship hovered silently above baby dog while G was ticking off the checklist items one by one.

Baby dog checklist:

1. Bark with a 'woof woof' sound ✓
2. Wag its small tail often ✓
3. White colored with brown patches ✓

"Yes! Yes! Yes! Hooray! ZAP!", shouted Alien G as all the checklist items matched. G pressed the ZAP button on the console, and the baby dog was instantly sucked into the spaceship.

B and G locked up the baby dog in the same cage

as Mrs. Dog. The aliens celebrated their success by

doing a high five. Mrs. Dog and the baby dog were

very sad, as just some time back they were free,

happily strolling in the garden and playing in the

park respectively, and all of a sudden, they got

locked up in a cage. Mrs. Dog and the baby dog

started praying for some miracle to get out of the

cage and return home.

The aliens now only needed two more pairs of

animals before they could go back home. They

eagerly started looking for the next animal. In a

nearby jungle, they spotted a fox that was relaxing

under a tree. The aliens were not aware of the

fox's excellent sense of hearing and the moment

they neared it, the fox leaped to its feet and

started running. But G was too fast and pressed the

ZAP button quickly and the next instant the fox was

lifted into the spaceship.

B and G were very happy with their third catch.

"Good day, strange animal. I'm B and this is G, may I know who you are?", asked B. "I'm Mr. Fox", replied the fox.

"Nice meeting you, Mr. Fox! We have a science exhibition on our planet, and we must bring three unique pairs of adult and baby animals. We'll put you and baby fox on display there. Alongside dog and baby dog, you'll be the star attractions there!", beamed B.

The aliens locked him up in a cage and Mr. Fox became unhappy. G's eyes surveyed the animal from top to bottom and she keyed the following details into her laptop,

Baby fox checklist:

1. Have big pointy ears
2. Have a large bushy tail
3. Reddish orange colored

Mr. Fox did not care an iota about becoming a star attraction at the cost of his freedom. He started studying the surroundings carefully as he thought of an escape plan.

Baby fox was having so much fun playing run and catch with his friend.

After playing for some time, baby fox became thirsty and went to the pond to have a drink.

The alien spaceship hovered silently above baby fox while G was ticking off the checklist items one by one.

Baby fox checklist:

1. Have big pointy ears ✔
2. Have a large bushy tail ✔
3. Reddish orange colored ✔

"Yes! Yes! Yes! Yahoo! ZAP!", shouted G, and the baby fox was pulled into the spaceship.

B and G locked up the baby fox together with Mr. Fox. The aliens again celebrated their success by doing a high five. They now needed only one more adult-child animal pair and then they could start their return journey home.

Baby fox became very sad and started crying. It wanted to go back to the jungle and play with its friend. Mr. Fox asked baby fox not to worry as he had just thought of a wonderful idea for their escape.

FOX AND CUB

Mr. Fox called the aliens over and said," Dear B and G, you only need one more pair of animals to complete your mission. But there is not much uniqueness between dogs and foxes. We are so closely related and have many things in common, it is even possible some people may mistake us for the same."

FOX AND CUB

"Mr. Fox, what do you suggest?", asked B with an anxious face. "Let me suggest a wonderful and unique animal so that everyone in your school will applaud and you'll be sure to win the first prize in the exhibition", said Fox. On hearing this, both B and G started melting like butter under the sun and thanked Mr. Fox.

Mr. Fox had asked the aliens to go to the edge of the Amazon rainforest to capture a flamingo. The alien spaceship was now hovering over a flamboyance of flamingos. The aliens found that the flamingos were stunningly beautiful and G pressed the ZAP button immediately and the next instant a flamingo was hauled into the spaceship.

B and G were very happy with their fifth catch and B thanked Mr. Fox as the flamingo was both beautiful and also looked very much different from Mrs. Dog and Mr. Fox.

"Good day, Flamingo. We have a science exhibition on our planet, and we must bring three unique pairs of adult and baby animals. We'll put you and the baby flamingo on display there. Alongside dog and fox, you'll be the star attraction there!", said B.

The flamingo became dismal and the aliens locked it in a big cage. G examined the flamingo from top to bottom and logged the following details into her laptop,

Baby flamingo checklist:

1. Long, slender legs
2. Long, curvy neck
3. Pink colored

The aliens now only needed to capture the baby flamingo and then their mission would be accomplished. They started searching the neighborhood for baby flamingos. They hovered on top of a baby flamingo and G started ticking off her checklist,

Baby flamingo checklist:

1. Two long, slender legs ✔
2. Long, curvy neck ✔
3. Pink colored ✖

"Yes! Yes! and………No!?!", mumbled G. The baby bird was dull grey colored instead of the beautiful pink they were looking for and the aliens decided it should be some other animal. They started searching for baby flamingos in other places.

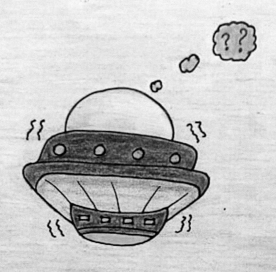

In search of a baby flamingo, the aliens make one complete orbit around the Earth but still, they could not find any baby animal that matched their baby flamingo checklist. B and G get tired, halt their search, and free the adult flamingo from its cage.

Behind the aliens' backs, Mr. Fox and baby fox high

paw each other. Baby fox was now confident that

Mr. Fox would save him from the aliens and

awaited eagerly to see what other tricks Mr. Fox

had under his sleeve.

FOX AND CUB

Alien B said to the fox," It is quite strange Mr. Fox, we've searched everywhere but cannot find a baby flamingo". "Dear B, it might just be bad timing, maybe all the baby flamingos are taking a nap inside their homes. Don't worry. I've thought of a wonderful 4-legged herbivorous animal that you'll like.", replied Mr. Fox.

The aliens brightened up and based on Mr. Fox's directions, they flew to a dense forest in Malaysia to look for the Malayan Tapir. The spaceship hovered over a strange-looking animal that looked slightly like an elephant but only much smaller with a round barrel-shaped body, short legs, and stubby tail. Upon Mr. Fox's confirmation, G pressed the ZAP button, and the next instant the heavy tapir was heaved up into the spaceship.

B and G were very happy with their catch and as usual, B started talking to the Tapir and G started taking notes. Alien B explained to the Tapir why they were abducting it and locked it inside the cage. The tapir looked glum as G studied it from top to bottom and recorded the following details into her laptop,

Baby tapir checklist:

1. Short trunk for reaching and plucking leaves & fruits
2. Stubby tail
3. Color: Black at the front and back, white in the middle

The aliens now only needed to capture the baby Tapir and then they could return to Planet Qurious. They started searching the neighborhood for baby Tapir. They found something similar and hovered on top of a baby tapir while G started ticking off her checklist.

Baby tapir checklist:

1. Short trunk for reaching and plucking leaves & fruits ✔

2. Stubby tail ✔

3. Color: Black at the front and back, white in the middle ✘

"Yes! Yes! and.........No, not again!", shouted G. The baby tapir was covered in black and white stripes and spots instead of the distinct black-white-black color columns they were looking for, and the aliens decided it was some other animal. They continued their search in other places.

The aliens make one full revolution around the Earth but they still could not find the baby tapir based on their checklist. B and G become very tired, stop their search, and free the adult tapir from its cage.

Behind the aliens' backs, Mr. Fox and baby fox again high paw each other.

Alien B said to the fox," It is strange yet again Mr. Fox, we've searched everywhere but cannot find baby Tapir."

"Dear B, I suppose it is just wrong timing, maybe all the baby tapirs are underwater as they like to use their trunk as snorkel and play underwater. Don't worry. I've thought of a wonderful 6-legged, brightly colored, vibrant, and graceful animal that is sure to get everyone excited at your school.", replied Mr. Fox.

Based on Fox's suggestion, the spaceship was now hovering over a beautiful kaleidoscope of Monarch butterflies. G pressed the ZAP button and in the next instant, a butterfly was uplifted into the spaceship.

Though tired, B and G were happy and satisfied with their catch as the Monarch butterfly was a very beautiful creature and the aliens had never seen anything quite like it before. Alien B explained to the Butterfly why they were abducting it and below are the observation notes from G's laptop,

Baby butterfly checklist:

1. Lightweight and flies most of the time

2. Extendable and retractable long straw-like mouth to drink nectar from flowers

3. Two pairs of brilliant orange-red wings

The aliens start searching for the baby butterfly. They started with the neighborhood first but all they could find were some caterpillars hungrily munching on some leaves.

Baby butterfly checklist:

1. Lightweight and flies most of the time ✖

2. Extendable and retractable long straw-like mouth to drink nectar from flowers ✖

3. Two pairs of brilliant orange-red wings ✖

"No! No! and......... Noooooo!", cried G. The aliens decided it was not possible for the slow-crawling worm-like creature to be in any way related to the graceful and beautiful butterfly and decided to continue their search elsewhere.

The aliens are quite desperate now and make THREE complete rounds around the Earth to do a thorough search but they could not find any baby animal closest to the Monarch butterfly.

B and G are completely exhausted and stop their search. Behind the aliens' backs, Mr. Fox and baby fox high paw each other.

Suddenly, there is a loud warning beep sound in the spaceship, and the aliens check out the warning notification and find that the fuel is nearing empty and they only have just enough remaining to return to Planet Qurious. **"UH-OH!"**, exclaimed both the aliens.

"Dear animals of Earth, we must abort our mission now as our fuel is nearing empty. We will take Mrs. Dog and baby dog, Mr. Fox and baby fox to our planet and release the rest of you back to Earth as we cannot find your babies.", announced B.

Mr. Fox had anticipated such a scenario and replied," Dear B, your fuel is near empty and it would be a huge risk to take any additional cargo. Any additional weight on board will deplete the fuel faster and you may end up getting stranded in the middle of nowhere and not reach Planet Qurious. It would be better for you to release all of the captured animals and have a pleasant worry-free journey."

What Mr. Fox had said about the link between fuel consumption and weight was true and G recalled this fact from her Physics class. After discussing it among themselves, B and G agreed that it was best for them to leave immediately and not carry any extra cargo. So, they released all the captured animals safely back to Earth.

All the animals were very happy and thanked Mr. Fox for using his wit to outfox the aliens and win their freedom.

~ End of story ~

FIND THE CORRECT SEQUENCE

1.
2.
3.
4.

Correct Sequence: 4, 1, 2, 3

Match the below animal with the correct term that is referred to call a group of them.

1. Flamingo
2. Leopard
3. Butterfly
4. Kangaroo
5. Fox
6. Caterpillar

a. mob
b. skulk
c. flamboyance
d. leap
e. army
f. kaleidoscope

Answers: 1. c, 2. d, 3. f, 4. a, 5. b, 6. e

Please turn to page 57 for answers

49

FASCINATING ANIMAL FACTS

- Arctic foxes **change their fur color** depending on the season. In the winter, their fur morphs into the iconic, thick white coating. But as summer arrives, Arctic foxes start to shed their long white coat to a shorter, thinner fur, that is grey or brown colored.

- You're invisible, but I'll eat you anyway: Foxes have an **impeccable hearing** - it's reported that red foxes can hear a watch ticking from 40 yards away! The above-ground fox can dive and catch an underground mouse that is buried 3 feet down.

- **Great parents:** Flamingos generally produce one egg annually, which both parents take turns to incubate. Young chicks receive nourishment known as crop milk from both the mother and father.

- **You are what you eat:** Baby flamingos are born gray or white. They usually turn pink within the first couple of years of life. Flamingos get their pink color from their food. Carotenoids are found in the microscopic algae that brine shrimp eat. As a flamingo dines on algae and brine shrimp, its body metabolizes the pigments — turning its feathers pink.

- Flamingos are **filter-feeders** - in that respect, they resemble whales and oysters more than they do most birds.

- Malayan tapirs are also called **"Oreo" tapirs** because their distinctive black and white color pattern resembles an Oreo cookie.

- **Snorkelling:** Tapirs are excellent swimmers. They can hold their breath for as long as 3 minutes and walk along the bottom of riverbeds, like hippos, searching for plants to graze on. Their unique snout helps tapirs reach and grab their food and also acts as a snorkel when tapirs swim underwater.

- Baby tapirs are born with black and white stripes and spots, a pattern that enables them to stay **camouflaged** in the thick rainforest.

- Tapirs are known as the **"gardeners of the forest"** because they eat diverse plants and fruits. They disperse the seeds in their dung, helping forests regenerate.

- The butterfly lays eggs which hatch into caterpillars, which eat quite a lot and grow quickly. Once the caterpillar has reached its required growth, it forms itself into a chrysalis. Once inside the chrysalis, it undergoes a transformation called **metamorphosis** and emerges as a beautiful adult butterfly that does not grow further in size.

- Butterflies don't have tongues and **taste with their feet**. They don't have teeth and feed on liquid food by sucking nectar/juice from flowers/fruits using their long straw-like mouth.

RIDDLE TIME!

1. It's counting time - how many "A"s are there in the sentence "An army of caterpillars"?

2. Mrs. Dog was on one side of the river, and her pup was playing on the other side. There was no bridge or boat. Mrs. Dog told the pup, "It is getting late kiddo, let's go home, come on!" The pup crossed the river and they both walked home. However, the pup did not get wet - how can that be?

3. A quick brown fox jumps over the lazy dog – what is special about this sentence?

4. What does this say?
   Mr. Fox was YY 4 the aliens!

5. Some books start at the end and go backward in time. Can you think of a popular book where the chicken comes before the egg?

6. What do you call a group of cattle with a sense of humor?

7. Imagine a bridge 2 Kilometers long and strong enough to hold exactly 11000 Kilograms, it will collapse if there is any more weight. A loaded truck weighing exactly 11000 Kilograms drives onto the bridge. A kaleidoscope of butterflies weighing 2 grams land on the truck at the halfway point, yet the bridge does not collapse. How is this possible?

8. What animal sound goes around and around a tree?

9. What has a bed but never sleeps, has a mouth but never eats, always runs but never walks, often murmurs but never talks?

10. The alphabet goes from A to Z but I go from Z to A. What am I?

Please turn to page 57 for answers

Dear kids, can you develop the below hints into a short story?

Hungry fox – ripe, plump grapes – cannot reach – think – idea – roll a hollow log – jump from it – can reach – delicious.

ANSWERS SECTION

Can you spot 8 differences?

Cloud, extra bird in the sky, spaceship light, bush, flamingo eating fish, stones near the pond, extra fish near lotus, plant near lotus.

Riddles:

1. There is only one "A"; the others are lowercase "a".

2. The river was frozen.

3. It is an English-language pangram —
   a sentence containing all the alphabet.

4. Mr. Fox was too wise for the aliens!

5. The dictionary.

6. Laughing stock.

7. The truck would have burnt off more than 2g of fuel during the first 1km ride to reach the middle of the bridge. So, the total weight of the truck is still within the bridge's threshold.

8. Bark.

9. A river.

10. A zebra

AUTHOR'S NOTE

Aliens Outfoxed is my second book and I hope to publish more! Just like Mr. Fox, treasure your freedom and fight for your loved ones' freedom and happiness. There are different forms of fighting and keep the violent form as a last resort as in most situations, a calm and clear mind will see you through!

     I was lucky to have an amazing school Principal (Mr. P. Ramaiah) and below is one of the many motivational songs he made us sing during the morning assembly sessions.

A few lines from George Baker's Paloma Blanca song (1975)

When the sun shines on the mountain
And the night is on the run
It's a new day, it's a new way
And I fly up to the sun
Una paloma blanca
I'm just a bird in the sky
Una paloma blanca
Over the mountains, I fly
No one can take my freedom away
Yes, no one can take my freedom away

Use your time to do what you love and pursue what gives you happiness.

Love and regards,
Vimal
(Vimal.april@gmail.com)

Made in United States
North Haven, CT
19 September 2023

41624146R10033